The Maestro Plays

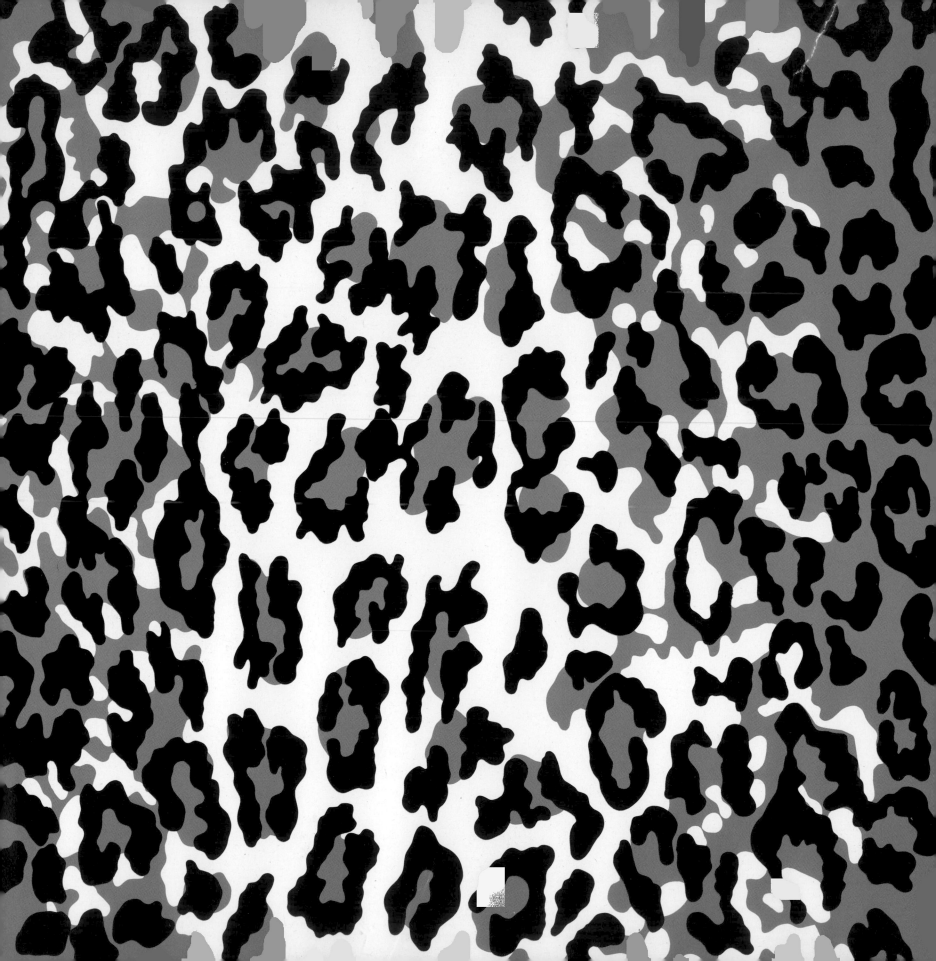

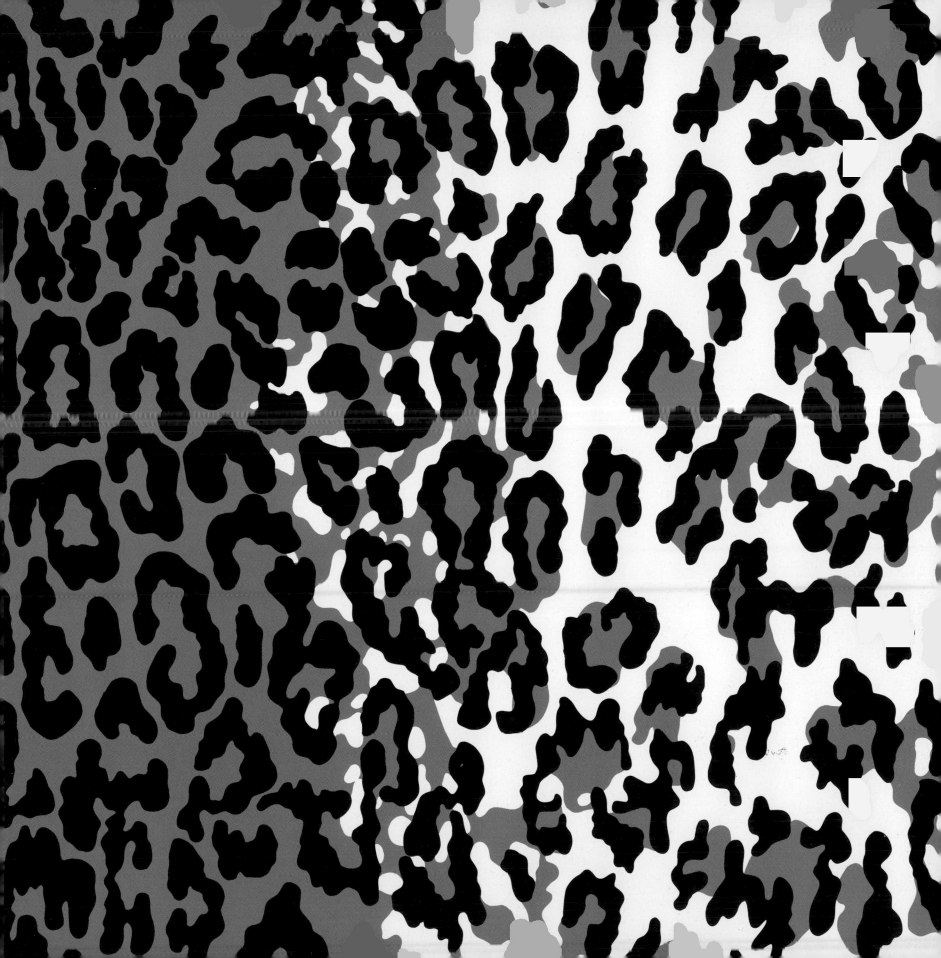

The Maestro Plays

First Voyager Books edition 1996
Voyager Books is a registered trademark of
Harcourt Brace & Company.

Library of Congress Cataloging-in-Publication Data
Martin, Bill, 1916—
The maestro plays/by Bill Martin Jr; illustrated by
Vladimir Radunsky.
p.   cm.
"Voyager books."
Summary: Pictures accompany a brief rhyming text
describing the antics and sounds of a musician's recital.
ISBN 0-15-201217-6
[1. Musicians—Fiction. 2. Stories in rhyme.] I. Radunsky,
Vladimir, ill. II. Title.
[PZ8.3.M418Mae 1996]
[E]—dc20   95-49126

ISBN 0-15-201217-6

A C E D B

Printed and bound by Tien Wah Press, Singapore
This book was printed with soya-based inks on Leykam
recycled paper, which contains more than 20 percent
postconsumer waste and has a total recycled content of at
least 50 percent.

Printed in Singapore

Voyager Books   Harcourt Brace & Company   San Diego   New York   London

The Maestro Plays

by Bill Martin Jr

pictures by
Vladimir Radunsky

THE MAESTRO PLAYS.
HE PLAYS PROUDLY.
HE PLAYS LOUDLY.

He plays slowly

He plays oh..ly.

He plays reachingly.

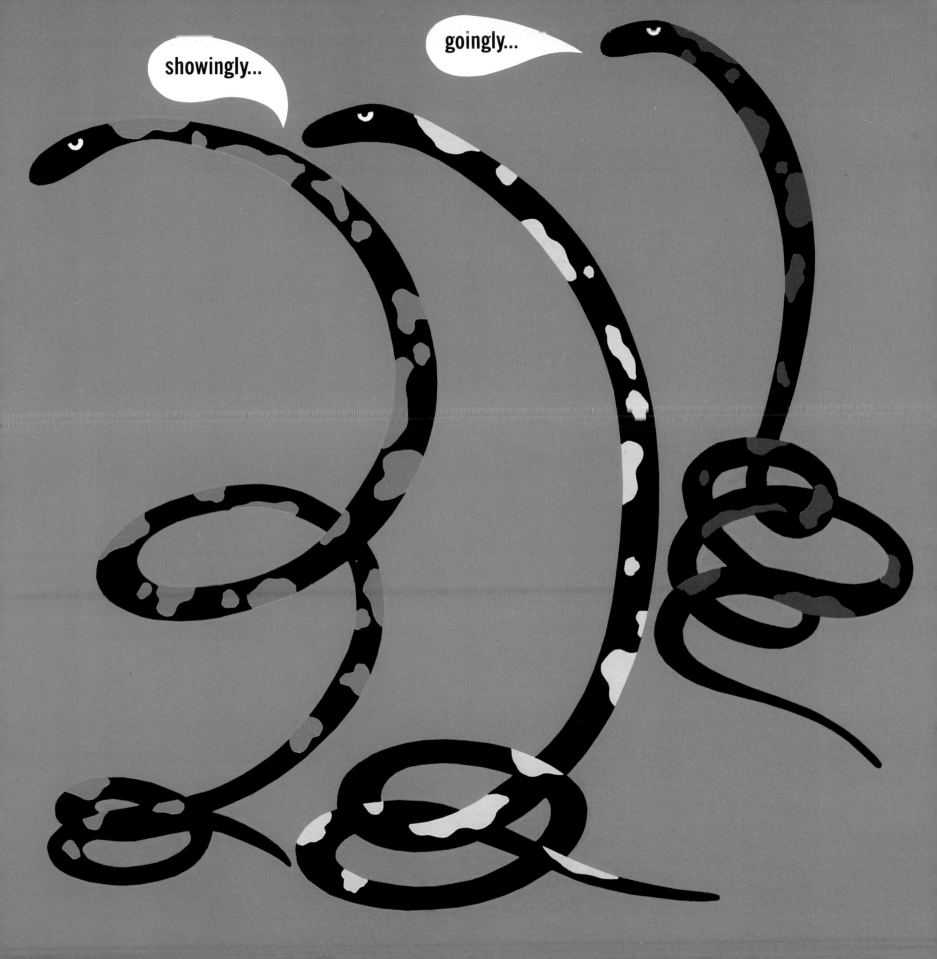

Now he is playing singingly.

He is playing ringingly,

wingingly . . .

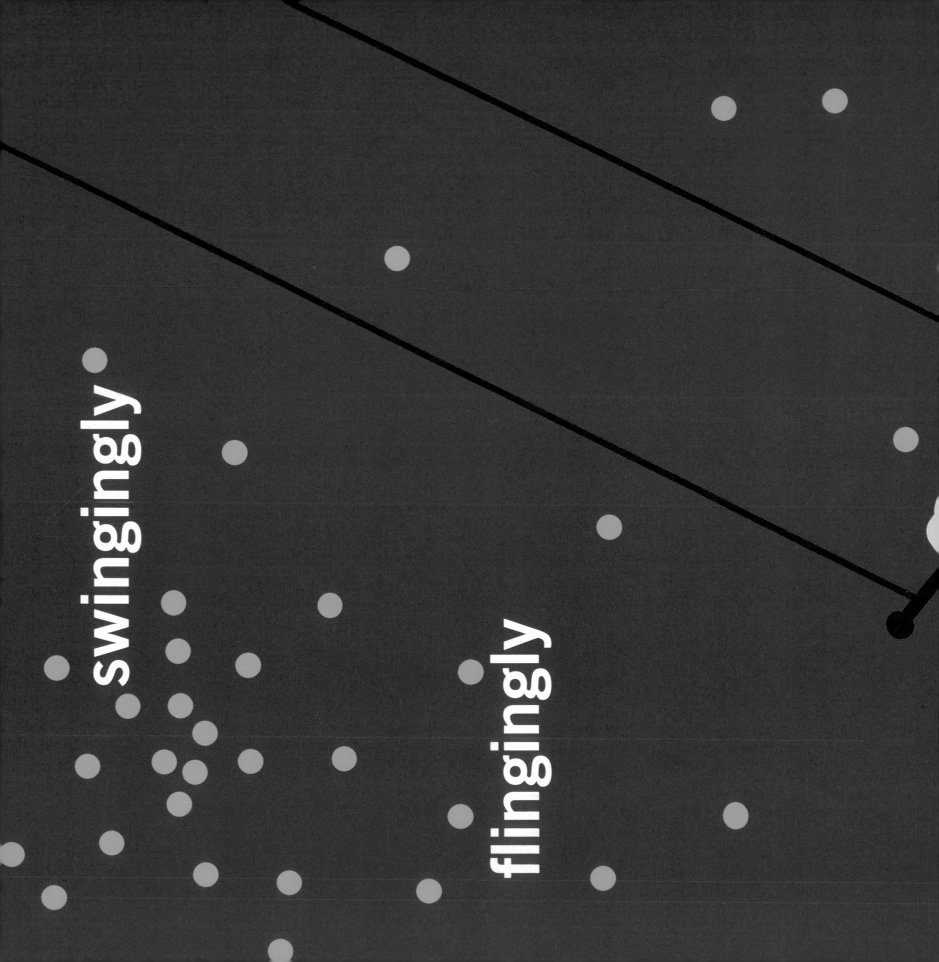

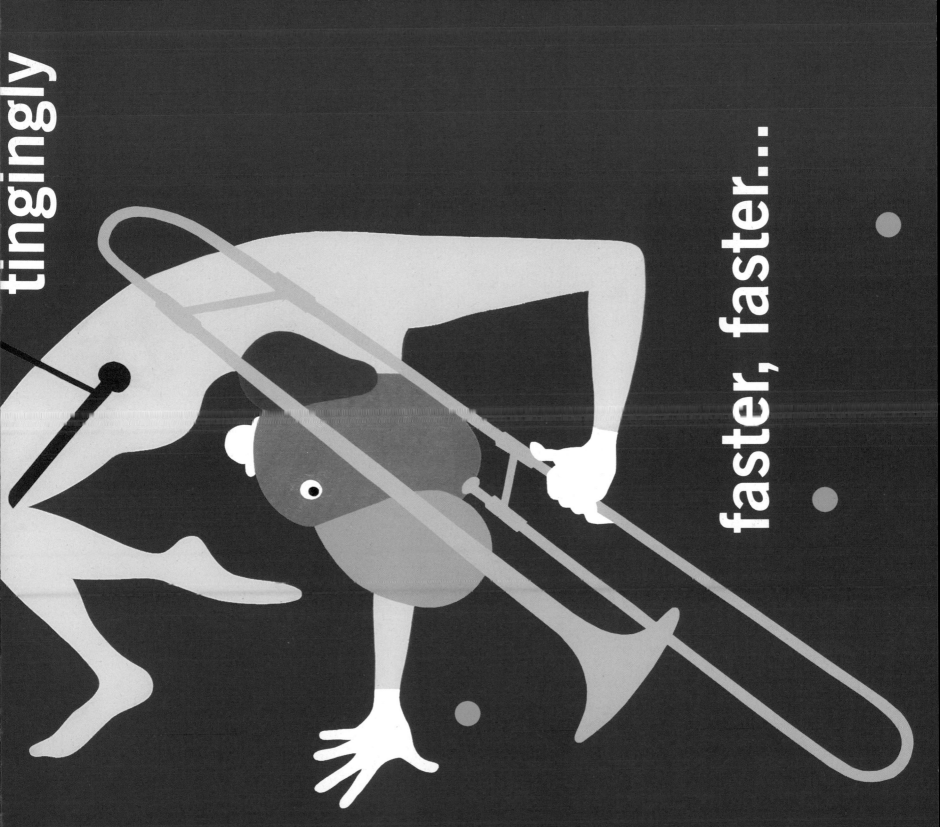

He plays busily.

He plays

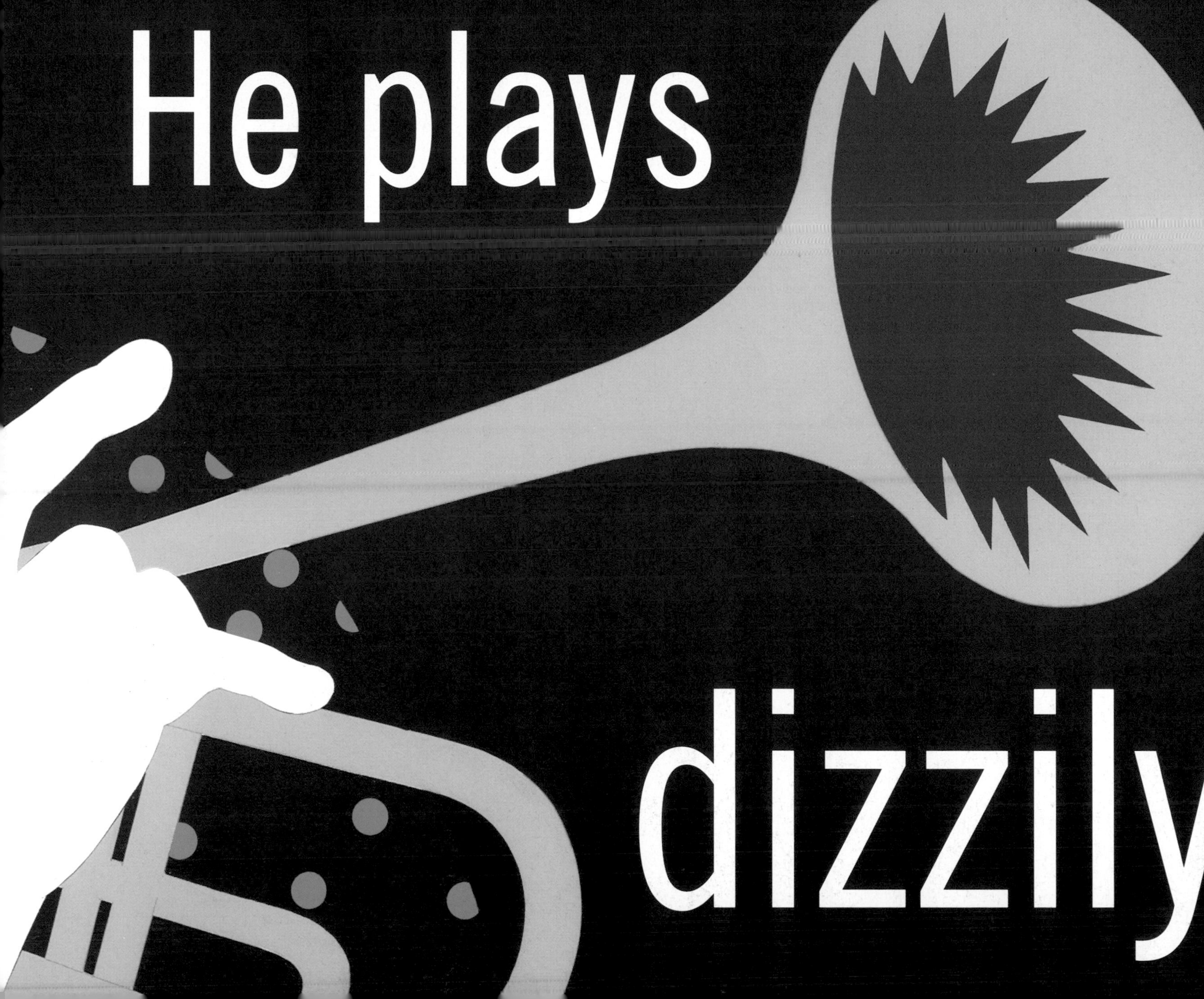

dizzily.

He stops. He mops his brow.

The maestro begins

playing again mildly....

But suddenly he's playing wildly...

He bows furiously

He jabs!

He stabs!

He saws!

He slaps the strings.

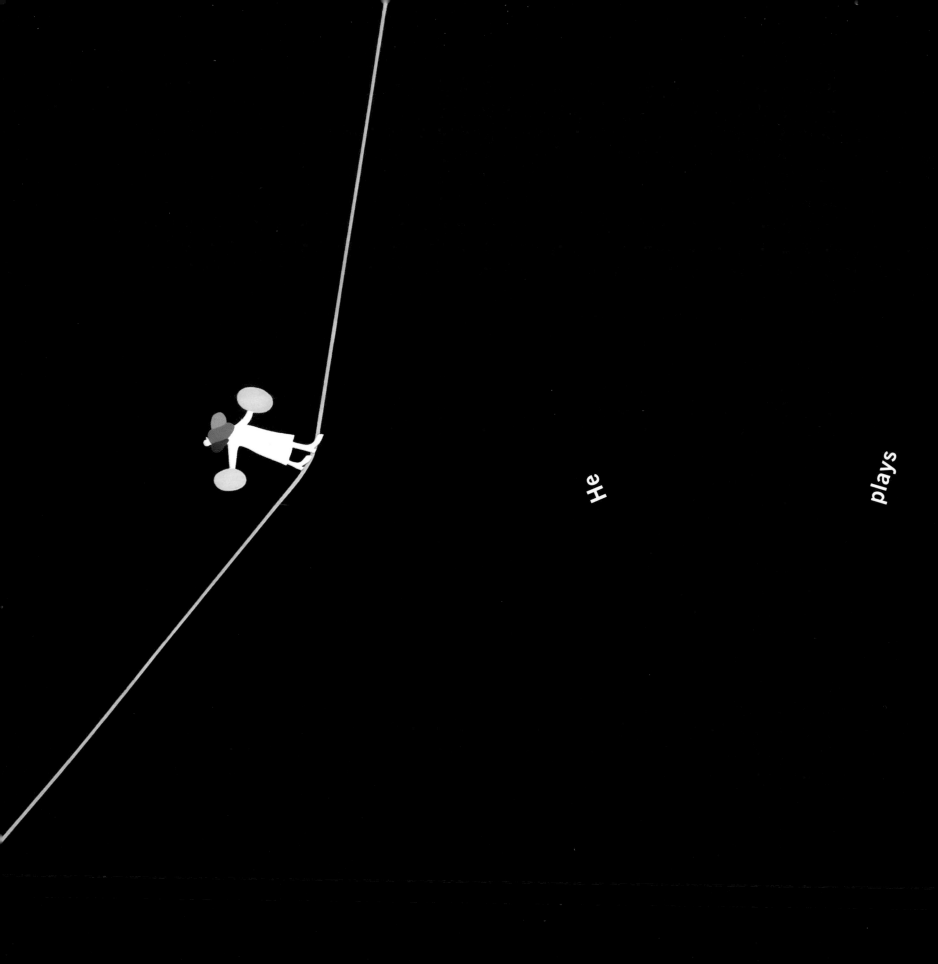

He plays

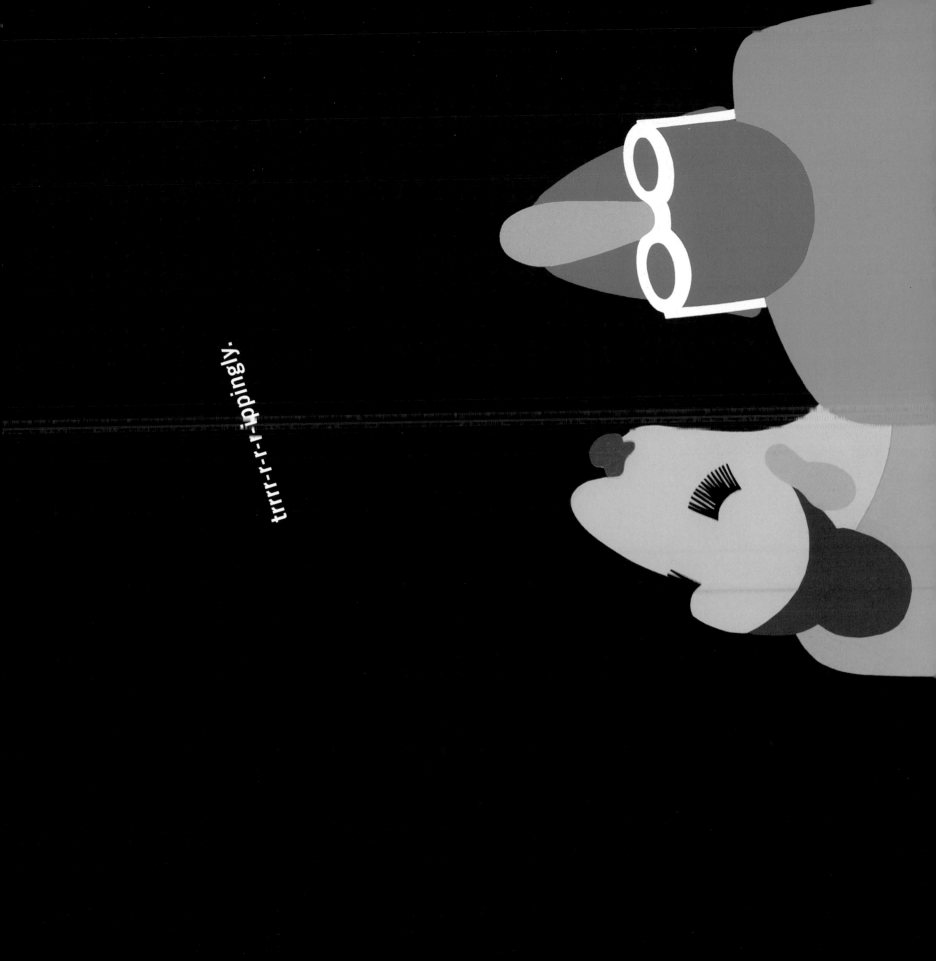

trrrr-r-r-r-ippingly.

He plays skippingly...

He plays sweepingly...
leapingly...
cheepingly...
faster...
faster.

He plays nippingly,

drippingly...

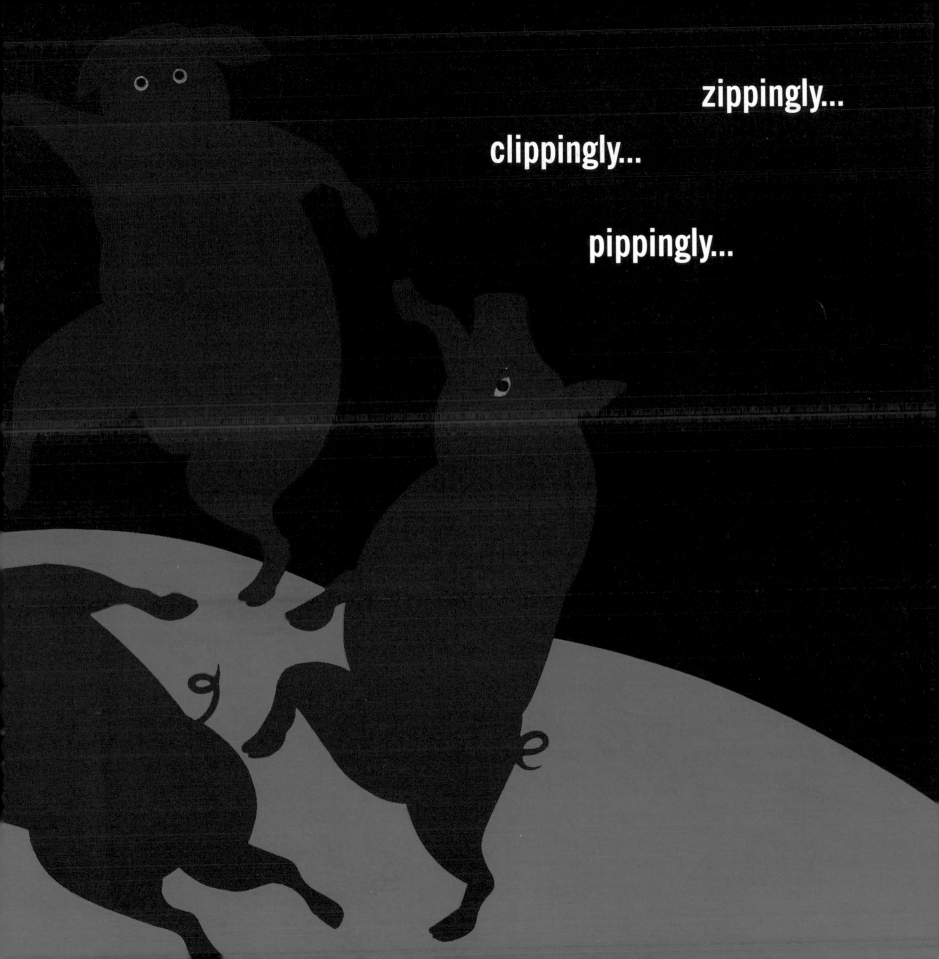

zippingly...

clippingly...

pippingly...

Rrrrriiiiiiiippppppiiinngly...

The concert is
over.